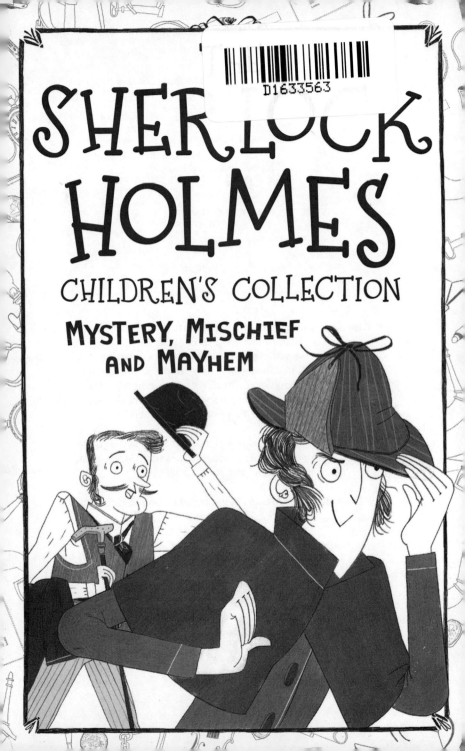

Published by Sweet Cherry Publishing Limited
Unit 36, Vulcan House,
Vulcan Road,
Leicester, LE5 3EF
United Kingdom

First published in the UK in 2020
2021 edition

2 4 6 8 10 9 7 5 3

ISBN: 978-1-78226-421-7

Sherlock Holmes: The Copper Beeches

Cover design by Arianna Bellucci and Rhiannon Izard
Illustrations by Arianna Bellucci

Lexile® code numerical measure L = Lexile® 710L

Guided Reading Level = W

www.sweetcherrypublishing.com

Printed and bound in India
I.TP002

SHERLOCK HOLMES

THE COPPER BEECHES

SIR ARTHUR CONAN DOYLE

Chapter One

I could tell that Sherlock Holmes was in a bad mood. He was restless, rattling his newspaper and puffing on his pipe.

We were sitting either side of a cheery fire, having just finished our breakfast. I was writing up one of Holmes' recent cases in my notebook. I chuckled from time to time as I remembered our adventure.

This seemed to annoy Holmes even more.

It was a cold day in early spring. As I glanced out of the window a thick fog rolled down the street, blocking my view of the other houses.

Holmes had been silent all morning, his head buried in the pages of a pile of newspapers. Then, suddenly giving up his search, he threw down the papers he had been reading and looked at me.

'I'm pleased to see, Watson, that you have written about my cases quite well.'

I smiled. 'And yet you have criticised my articles. You said that they were overdramatic.'

Holmes took a glowing coal from the fire using the tongs. He pressed it to his pipe, to relight it. 'You have certainly added colour and life where none existed.'

His arrogance annoyed me. 'I think I have done a good job.'

'No, it's not arrogance,' Holmes said, reading my mind.

'I am simply saying that the world could be a better place if everyone focussed more on logic, like me. I think your articles should inspire that in people. You have turned what should have been a set of serious reports into a collection of fairy stories.'

I said nothing. I was afraid that I would seriously harm our friendship if I spoke my thoughts – some of them had been simmering for a while.

'But I suppose I cannot blame you. The days of the great cases are past. Criminals have lost their creativity and originality.'

He picked up a letter from the table. 'As to my own little business, it has become nothing more than an agency for finding lost pencils and giving advice to love-struck young ladies. I think I have hit rock bottom at last. The note I had this morning marks a new low. Read it!'

The note he tossed to me was crumpled as if he had screwed it up to fling into the bin, but then thought better of it. Perhaps he

had kept it just to make
this point.

Montague Place
Tuesday 18th March, 1890

Dear Mr Holmes,
I am very anxious to consult you. I
would like to know whether I should
or should not accept a job that has
been offered to me as a governess.
I shall call at half-past ten tomorrow.

Yours faithfully,
Violet Hunter

'How strange! Do you know this young lady?' I asked.

'No.'

I glanced at the clock on the mantelpiece. 'It is half-past ten now.'

'Yes, and I have no doubt that that is her,' he said, as the doorbell rang below.

'It may turn out to be more interesting than you think,' I said. 'The affair of the Blue Carbuncle seemed such a silly, almost boring case at first, but it developed into a serious investigation. It may be the same with this case, too.'

'Well, let us hope so. Either way we'll know very soon, for here is the person in question.'

As he spoke, the door opened and Mrs Hudson showed in our visitor.

Chapter Two

A young lady entered, plainly but neatly dressed, with a bright, alert, freckled face. She had the brisk manner of a woman who has had to make her own way in the world.

'I'm sorry to trouble you,' she said, as Holmes rose to greet her, 'but I have had a very strange experience. And, as I have no parents or relatives to advise me,

I thought you might be kind enough to help.'

'Please take a seat, Miss Hunter. I shall be happy to do anything I can to help you.'

I was surprised at Holmes' eagerness to help, but could see that he was impressed by her direct manner and speech. These were traits he liked. After looking at her curiously, he settled himself in his chair and pressed his fingertips together, ready to listen to her story.

I sat to one side,

14

where I could listen and observe.

'I have been a governess for five years,' she began, 'for the family of Colonel Spence Munro. Two months ago, the colonel was posted to Halifax in Nova Scotia, Canada. He took his children with him, so I found myself without a job. I advertised, but had no success.

'At last, the little money I had saved was running out. I was at my wits' end as to what I should do.'

Holmes nodded to show that he was listening and to encourage her to continue.

'There is a well-known agency for governesses in London called Westaways. I used to call there once a week to see whether any suitable jobs had turned up. It is managed by a Miss Stoper, who sits in a little office and interviews the ladies, one by one. She looks at her books and sees whether she has any jobs that would suit them.

'Well, when I called last week I was shown into the little office, as usual, but I found that Miss Stoper was not alone. Her visitor was a fat man with a smiling face and a great, heavy chin. He sat beside her, peering through his glasses as I entered. I could see that he had been watching every lady who came in. He looked as if he was getting tired. But as soon as he saw me, he jumped up from his chair and turned quickly to Miss Stoper.

"'That will do!" he said. "I could not ask for anything better!" He seemed very pleased and rubbed his hands together, still smiling broadly. His face was pleasant to look at.

"'Are you looking for a job, miss?" he asked.

"'Yes, sir."

"'As a governess?"

"'Yes, sir."

"'And what salary do you ask for?"

"'I was paid four pounds a month in my last job, with

Colonel Spence Munro."

"'Oh, tut, tut!" he cried, throwing his fat hands into the air. "How could anyone offer so little money to a lady with such beauty and talents?"

"'My talents, sir, may be less than you imagine," I said. "A little French, a little German, music and drawing ..."

"'Tut, tut!" he cried again. "This is all quite beside the question. The point is, have you the posture and manner of a lady? That is it in a nutshell.

If you have not, then you are not suitable to bring up a child. Particularly a child who is destined for great things. But if you have, how could any gentleman pay you any less than a three-figure sum? Your salary with me, madam, would begin at a hundred pounds a year.'"

At this, Holmes' eyes widened and I sat up in my chair. The story had just become much more interesting. Why would anyone pay such a high salary for what seemed to be an ordinary job?

'You may imagine, Mr Holmes, that to me such an offer seemed too good to be true. The gentleman must have seen the look of disbelief on my face because he opened up his wallet and took out a five pound note.

'"It is also my habit," he said, smiling so broadly that his eyes became no more than two shining slits, "to give my young ladies part of their salary in advance. It will pay for your journey and new clothes."

'It seemed to me that I had never met such a kind or thoughtful man. As I was already in debt, the money was a godsend. On the other hand, there was something unnatural about the whole thing. It made me wish to know a little more before I accepted the job.'

I saw Holmes nod in agreement and I thought her very wise, too.

'I asked him where he lived.

'"In Hampshire," he replied. "Charming rural place. The

Copper Beeches it's called. Five miles from Winchester. It is the most lovely countryside, my dear young lady, and the dearest old house."

"'And my duties, sir? I should like to know what they will be."

"'One child. One dear little rascal, who's just six years old. Oh, if you could see him killing cockroaches with a slipper! Smack! Smack! Smack! Three gone before you could wink." He leaned back in his chair and laughed heartily.

"'My only duties then," I asked, "are to take care of a single child?"

"'No, no, that is not your only duty, my dear young lady," he cried. "Your duty will be to obey any little commands my wife might give. That won't be difficult, eh?"

"'I would be happy to make myself useful."

"'Quite so. In dress, for example, we are particular people. Particular, but kind-hearted. If you were asked to wear any clothes that we might give you, you would not refuse? Heh?"

"'No,' I said, very surprised at his words.

"'Or if you were asked to sit here or sit there, that would not trouble you?'"

"'Oh, no.'"

"'Or to cut your hair quite short?'"

Holmes leaned forwards, frowning. 'To cut your hair?'

'I could hardly believe my ears, Mr Holmes.' She looked at each of us in turn.

'You may see that I have thick, shiny hair, in a rich chestnut colour. I have been complimented on it many times. I could not dream of giving it up for no good reason.

'Of course, I told him that it was quite impossible. He had been watching me eagerly out of his small eyes, and I saw a shadow pass over his face as I spoke.

'"I'm afraid it is essential," he said. "It is a little idea of my wife's. When she gets an idea in her head she will not let it go. You're sure you won't cut your hair?"

'"No, sir, I really could not," I answered firmly.

'"Ah, very well. Then that settles the matter. It is a pity because you would have been just right for the job. In that case, Miss Stoper, I had better see a few more of your young ladies."

'Miss Stoper looked up at me angrily – I suspect my refusal had lost her a lot of money.

'"Do you wish your name to be kept on the books?" she asked.

'"Yes, please, Miss Stoper."

'"Well, there doesn't seem much point, since you have refused such an excellent offer," she said sharply. "You could hardly expect us to go to any trouble to find you another job. Good day to you, Miss Hunter."

'She struck a gong on the desk and I was shown out by a young boy.

'Well, Mr Holmes, when I got back home I found my kitchen cupboard empty and two or three bills lying on the table. I began to think I had been foolish. After all, these people may have strange requests, but they were going to pay well for their weirdness. Very few governesses in England are getting a hundred pounds a year. And what use was my hair to me? Maybe it would look good short. Within a couple of days, I was certain that I had made a mistake. I was almost ready to overcome my pride and go back to the agency. That was when I received a letter from the gentleman himself. I have it here. I will read it to you.'

She took a letter from an envelope and smoothed it out on her lap.

The Copper Beeches,
near Winchester
18th March, 1890

Dear Miss Hunter,
Miss Stoper very kindly gave me your address. I write to ask whether you have changed your mind. My wife is very keen that you should come — she was very impressed by my description of you. We are willing to give you one hundred and twenty pounds a year, if you agree to our little requests. They are not very demanding, after all.

My wife is fond of a particular shade of electric blue. She would like you to wear a dress in that colour, indoors, in the morning. You do not need to buy one. We have one that belonged to our dear daughter, Alice. She is now in Philadelphia, but I think the dress will fit you very well.

We may ask you to sit here or there, but that shouldn't be a problem to you.

As to your hair, it is a pity. I noticed its beauty during our short interview, but I'm afraid I must insist that you cut it short. I hope that the increased salary will pay for your loss.

Your duties, as far as the child is concerned, are very light.

Do try to come and I shall meet you with the dog-cart at Winchester. Let me know which train you are taking.

Yours faithfully,
Jephro Rucastle

'That is the letter that I have just received, Mr Holmes, and my mind is made up that I will accept it. I thought, however, that I should ask your opinion first.'

'Well, Miss Hunter, if your mind is made up, that answers the question,' said Holmes, smiling.

'But would you advise me to refuse?'

'I must say that it is not the kind of job I should like a sister of mine to apply for.'

'What is the meaning of it all, Mr Holmes?'

'Ah, I cannot tell. Perhaps you have formed some opinion?' He looked sharply at the young woman.

'Well, there seems to me to be only one possible solution. Mr Rucastle seemed to be a very kind, good-natured man. Perhaps his wife has some sort of mental illness and he prefers her to stay at home rather than go to a hospital. Maybe he humours her to keep her calm and happy.'

That thought had crossed my mind, too, and Holmes seemed to agree.

'That is a possible solution,' he said. 'In fact, it is the most likely one. But in any case, it does not seem to be a very nice household for a young lady.'

'But the money, Mr Holmes, the money!'

'Well, yes, of course, the pay is good … too good. That is what makes me uneasy. Why would they pay you a hundred and twenty pounds a year, when they could have their pick of governesses for forty? There must be a reason behind it.'

I was a little unsure myself, but Holmes seemed to be suspecting danger where there was none. Miss Hunter had told us Mr Rucastle was a kind gentleman and I trusted her judgement.

She replied, 'I thought that if I told you the details you would understand why I wanted your help. I would feel much better knowing I can turn to you for more advice, if I need it.'

'You are very wise. I assure you that your little problem promises to be the most interesting case that has come my way for some months. There is something very unusual about it. If you find yourself in any danger ...'

'Danger! What danger do you expect?'

Holmes shook his head. 'If we knew what to expect, there

wouldn't be anything dangerous about it,' he said. 'But at any time, day or night, a telegram would bring me at once.'

'That is enough for me,' she said, rising from her chair. All the worry had vanished from her face. 'I can happily move to Hampshire now. I shall write to Mr Rucastle at once, cut off my poor hair tonight, and leave for Winchester tomorrow.'

With a few grateful words, she said goodnight to us both and bustled off on her way.

I listened to her quick, firm steps descending the stairs. 'At least she seems able to look after herself,' I said.

'And she will need to do so,' said Holmes gravely. 'I am sure we shall hear from her soon.'

It was not long before my friend's prediction came true.

Chapter Three

Over the next few weeks, I often thought about Miss Hunter. I wondered what strange situation this lonely woman had wandered into. The unusual salary, the curious conditions, the light duties as far as teaching the boy. These all pointed to something abnormal. What could be the man's motive?

As to Holmes, I noticed that he often sat for half an hour at a time, with a frown on his face. But if I mentioned Violet Hunter, he swept the matter away with a wave of his hand.

'Information!' he said. 'Facts! I can't make bricks without clay!' And yet he would always finish by muttering that he would never have let his sister work in such a place.

The telegram came late one night. It was just as I was thinking of going to bed and Holmes was settling down for one of his all-night chemical experiments.

He opened the envelope and then, glancing at the message, threw it across to me.

'Please look up the trains in the Bradshaw,' he said. Then he turned back to his chemical studies.

The message was brief and urgent.

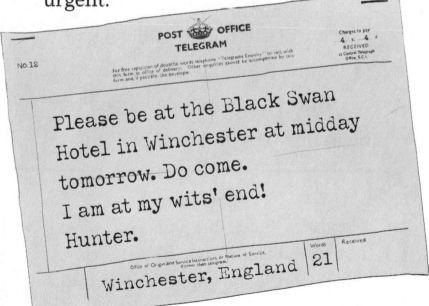

POST OFFICE
TELEGRAM

No. 12

Charges to pay
4 s. 4 d
RECEIVED
at Central Telegraph
Office, E.C.1.

For free repetition of doubtful words telephone "Telegrams Enquiry" or call with this form, at office of delivery. Other enquiries should be accompanied by this form and, if possible, the envelope.

Please be at the Black Swan Hotel in Winchester at midday tomorrow. Do come.
I am at my wits' end!
Hunter.

Office of Origin and Service Instructions or Nature of Service, if other than telegram.

Winchester, England

Words 21   Received

'Will you come with me?' asked Holmes, glancing up.

'I'd like to.'

'Just look up the trains then.'

'There is one at half-past nine,' I said, glancing over my Bradshaw. 'It is due to arrive at Winchester at eleven-thirty.'

'That will do nicely. Perhaps I'd better leave my chemical work and go to bed. We need to be at our best in the morning.'

Bradshaw

A Bradshaw Guide shows the exact times the trains will leave and arrive at each train station. It also gives some information about the area. Useful for staying ahead of the game!

By eleven o'clock the next day
we were on our way to Winchester.
Holmes had been absorbed in the
morning paper all the way, but after
we passed the Hampshire border
he threw it down and gazed out of
the window at the scenery. It was a
beautiful spring day. The light blue
sky was freckled
with little fleecy,
white clouds.

The sun was shining very brightly and yet there was a cool nip in the air, which I found energising. All over the countryside, little red and grey roofs of farmhouses peeped out from between the trees.

'Aren't they beautiful?' I cried, thinking how different the sweet little houses were to the cold brick walls of Baker Street.

But Holmes shook his head gravely.

'Do you know, Watson,' he said. 'That is one of the curses of having a brain like mine. I look at everything with my work in mind. You look at these houses, and you are impressed by their beauty. I look at them and only see how lonely they are, and how easy it would be to commit a crime here.'

'Good heavens!' I cried. 'Who would think of crime when looking at these dear old homes?'

'They always fill me with a certain dread.' Holmes seemed to give a slight shudder as he spoke. 'Based on my experience, Watson, more dreadful crimes occur in the smiling and beautiful countryside than in the darkest and dirtiest alleys in London.'

'You horrify me!'

'But the reason is very obvious. The sheer number of people and potential witnesses in large cities makes them much safer than the countryside. There is no lane in London where a child's scream would not be heard and worried about by the neighbours. The police are never far away, and it is only a step between the crime and the prison.

'But look at these lonely houses, each in its own field and filled with people who know little of the law. Think of the cruel deeds and hidden wickedness that can go on, year in, year out, in such places, and with no one the wiser.

'If the governess had gone to live in Winchester, I would not fear for her. It is the five miles

of countryside that makes the danger. Still, I do not think she is personally threatened.'

'Quite so. She has her freedom. What *can* be the matter then? Do you have an explanation?'

'I have thought of seven different explanations, each of which would cover the facts as we know them. We will only know which theory is correct when we get fresh information – which we will, no doubt, find waiting for us.'

'Well, we shall soon learn all that Miss Hunter has to tell.'

Chapter Four

The Black Swan was a pleasant
inn that sat in the high street,
very close to the station. There
we found the young lady waiting
for us. She had asked for a small
private room for our meeting. Our
lunch was waiting on the table.

'I am so delighted that you have
come,' she said. 'It is very kind of
you both. You see, I simply do not

know what to do – I desperately need your advice.'

We seated ourselves in the plush leather armchairs.

'Please tell us what has happened to you,' said Holmes.

'I will do so and I must be quick, for I have promised Mr Rucastle to be back before three o'clock. I got his permission to come into town this morning, though, of course, he does not know the reason.'

'Start at the beginning and tell us the whole story.' Holmes stretched his long, thin legs out towards the fire and settled himself to listen. I made myself comfortable, too.

'Firstly,' she began, 'I must say that I have had no bad treatment from either Mr or Mrs Rucastle. It is only fair to say that. But I cannot understand them, and I am worried about them.'

'What can you not understand?'

'The reason for their behaviour. When I arrived, Mr Rucastle met me here at the station and drove me, in his dog-cart, to The Copper Beeches. It is, as he said, a beautiful place, though the house itself is rather ugly. It is a large, square block of a house, painted white, but all stained and streaked with damp and bad weather.

'There are woods on three sides, and on the fourth side is a field. The ground in front belongs to the house, but the woods all around it are part of Lord Southerton's estate. A group of copper beech trees, which grow right outside the main door, has given the place its name.'

Dog-cart

A simple wooden cart drawn by one horse. These are often used to travel to and from big country houses. The rackety wheels will usually spray mud up the left-hand side of the cart. This makes it very easy to tell if someone has travelled by dog-cart, as they will have mud splats on their coat or shoes.

As she was describing the house, I was reminded of my conversation with Holmes on the train, and his worries about isolated places.

'I was driven to the house by Mr Rucastle, who was as friendly as ever. In the evening, he introduced me to his wife and the child. His wife was a silent, pale-faced woman, who was much younger than her husband.

He must be over forty-five. She could not be more than thirty, and she certainly did not seem mentally ill, as we thought.

'I think they have been married for about seven years. He was a widower and his only child by his first wife was the daughter who has gone to Philadelphia. Mr Rucastle told me in private that she left them because she didn't get on with his new wife. I imagine it was because they are so close in age.'

I relaxed a little at this – it's quite normal for a daughter not to like her young, new stepmother. And Mr and Mrs Rucastle seemed far less threatening than we had thought. But, then again, Miss Hunter had not yet explained the odd requests.

'Mrs Rucastle seems to have very little personality, though she does seem kind. It is easy to see that she loves her husband and her little son. Her light grey eyes are always looking at one or the other, checking to see they have everything they want. Mr Rucastle is kind to her, too, in his own way. On the whole they seem to be a happy couple. But I can tell she has some secret sorrow, this woman. She often sits lost in thought, with the saddest look on her face. More than once I have seen her crying when she didn't know I was there.

'I think it must be her son's behaviour that upsets her. I have never met such an utterly spoilt and naughty little boy. He is small for his age, and he is always either having a tantrum, or is gloomy and sulking. Causing pain to any creature weaker than himself

seems to be his only idea of fun.
He is very clever at catching mice,
little birds and insects and does
horrible things to them. But I
would rather not talk about this
child, Mr Holmes, as he has little
to do with my story.'

'No, no, please tell me all the
details,' said Holmes, 'whether
they seem to be important or not.'

'Well, apart from that horrid
boy, the one truly unpleasant
thing about the house is the staff.
There are only two; a man and
his wife. Toller is the man's name.

He is a rough, rude man, with grizzled hair and whiskers, and he always smells of alcohol. Twice already I have seen him quite drunk, yet Mr Rucastle doesn't take any notice of it.

'His wife is a very tall woman with a sour face. She is as silent as Mrs Rucastle but much less friendly. They are a horrible couple.

Fortunately, I spend most of my time in the nursery and my own room, so I don't have to see them very often.'

She paused for a moment. I took the opportunity to help myself to two of the tiny sandwiches from the table. It had been a long time since breakfast.

Holmes raised an eyebrow, but said nothing. I could not tell if he was being critical or not.

Miss Hunter quickly continued her tale. I tried to eat quietly to avoid interrupting her.

'For two days after my arrival at The Copper Beeches my life was very quiet. On the third day, Mrs Rucastle came down just after breakfast and whispered something to her husband.

'"Oh, yes," he said, turning to me. "We are very grateful, Miss Hunter, for you cutting your hair. I promise that it has not detracted the tiniest bit from your appearance."'

She glanced up at Holmes. Her expression told me that she was uncomfortable with the flattery.

'"Now we want to see how the electric blue dress suits you," Mr Rucastle said. "You will find it laid out on the bed in your room. If you would be so good as to put it on, we will both be very grateful."

'The dress was a funny shade of blue. It was a lovely material and fitted perfectly, but it showed signs of having been worn before. Both Mr and Mrs Rucastle were strangely excited when they saw me in it. We were in the drawing room, which is a very large room that stretches along the entire

front of the house.
It has three long
windows that reach
from the ceiling to
the floor.

'I was asked to
sit in a chair close
to the central
window, while Mr
Rucastle walked
up and down the
other side of the
room. He started
telling me some of
the funniest stories

that I had ever heard. You cannot imagine how funny he was – I laughed until my sides ached. Mrs Rucastle, however, never so much as smiled. As I said, she has very little personality. She sat with her hands in her lap and a sad look on her face.

'After an hour or so, Mr Rucastle suddenly stopped his stories. He then told me to change my dress and return to the nursery.

'Two days later we did the same thing again. I changed my dress, sat in the window and laughed at the funny stories Mr Rucastle told. He had so many of them and he told them so well. Then he handed me a yellow book and asked me to read aloud to him. I read for about ten minutes. Then, suddenly, in the middle of a sentence, he ordered me to stop and change my dress.

'You can imagine, Mr Holmes, how curious I became. What was the meaning of all of this? I noticed that they were always very careful to turn my face away from the window. I desperately

wanted to see what was going
on behind my back. At first it
seemed to be impossible, but I
soon thought up a plan. I had
broken my hand-mirror a couple
of days before, so I hid a piece
of it in my handkerchief. Then,
during the next storytelling, I
pretended to dab my eyes with
the handkerchief. That way
I could sneak a look at what
was behind me. Well, it was
very disappointing. There was
nothing … at first. On my second
glance, however, I saw that

there was a man
standing in the
road. He was a
small, bearded
man in a grey
suit. He seemed
to be looking in
my direction.

'I lowered my
handkerchief and
looked at Mrs Rucastle.
She was looking right at me!
She said nothing, but I am sure
that she knew what I was doing.
She got up at once.

"'Jephro,' she said, "there is a cheeky fellow in the road staring at Miss Hunter.'"

"'No friend of yours, Miss Hunter?' he asked.

"'No, I know no one in these parts.'

"'Dear me! How very rude! Please turn around and wave him away,' he replied.

"'Surely it would be better to take no notice?' I asked.

"'No, no. We don't want him hanging around here. Please turn around and wave him away.'"

'I did as I was told and Mrs Rucastle drew down the blind. That was a week ago. Since then I have not sat by the window again. Nor have I worn the blue dress, or seen the man in the road.'

'Please continue,' said Holmes, as he leaned in to choose a sandwich for himself. 'Your story promises to be very interesting.'

Chapter Five

'Well, I'm not sure this next part is connected at all, but I'll tell you anyway,' Miss Hunter continued. 'On the first day that I was at The Copper Beeches, Mr Rucastle took me to a small building, just outside the kitchen door. As we approached it I heard a chain rattling and a sound like a large animal moving about.

"Look in here!" said Mr Rucastle,

showing me a slit between two planks. "Is he not a beauty?"

'I looked through and saw the shape of a huge dog huddled in the darkness. Two eyes glowed from its massive head. I stepped back as it gave a low growl.

'"Don't be frightened," said Mr Rucastle, laughing at me. "It is only Carlo, my mastiff. I call him mine,

Mastiff

This breed of dog is very powerful. They usually have sharp teeth, large bodies and are extremely strong. A mastiff dog needs to be carefully trained and cared for, otherwise it could be vicious. It is most important of all to make sure that a mastiff is well fed. A hungry mastiff is not a creature you would want to meet!

but really old Toller is the only man who can do anything with him. We feed him once a day, and not too much, so that he is always a little hungry. Toller lets him loose every night, and heaven help any trespasser who gets in his way. For goodness sake don't ever leave the house at night for any reason. It's as much as your life is worth."

'It surprised me that old Toller would be able to control the huge dog. As I said, he is always drunk. He never shows much kindness to humans, let alone animals.

'But Mr Rucastle wasn't lying. Two nights later I happened to look out of my bedroom window at about two o'clock in the morning. It was a beautiful moonlit night, almost as bright as day. I was admiring the pretty scene, when I noticed something moving under the shadow of the copper beech trees.

As it walked out into the moonlight, I saw what it was. It was the giant dog, as big as a calf! It was light brown with saggy cheeks, a black nose and huge muscles that rippled as it walked. It moved slowly across the lawn and vanished into the shadows on the other side. It sent a chill to my heart.'

There was silence in the room as Holmes and I ran over the horrid facts in our minds. Outside, in the main room of the inn, I could hear voices chatting away, and the odd street vendor's voice rang through the window.

'Please do eat some of these delicious sandwiches, Miss Hunter. You haven't taken a bite,' said Holmes, waving his hand at the table of food.

Miss Hunter nodded and took a sandwich. She stared at it miserably but I could see that her mind was still on her story.

'As you know, I cut off my hair before I left London,' Miss Hunter continued, putting her sandwich down. 'I tied it together with a ribbon and put it in the bottom of my trunk.

'One evening, I was putting some of my clothes away in my room, and found a mysteriously locked drawer. I took out my bunch of keys and the very first one I tried was a perfect fit! I pulled the drawer open. There was only one thing in it, but I'm sure you would never guess what it was. It was my hair!'

'But it couldn't be – it wasn't possible. I opened my trunk and found *my* hair was exactly where I'd left it. I laid the two bunches side by side. They were identical in both colour and thickness. Isn't that extraordinary? I put the hair back in the drawer and said nothing to the Rucastles. I felt guilty for opening the drawer that they had locked.'

I could see that Holmes was adding this last detail to the list of facts. I was sure that while he listened, his brain was trying to piece the clues together, like a jigsaw puzzle.

'The locked drawer wasn't the only mystery, Mr Holmes. There was a whole section of the house that was completely deserted.

Even the door that led to it was locked. I didn't think it was too strange, at first.

'But, one day, as I went upstairs, I met Mr Rucastle coming out of that exact door. He had a terrifying look on his face. His cheeks were red and his brow was crinkled with anger, so that the veins stood out. He locked the door and hurried past me without a word.

'I couldn't help but be curious. That afternoon I went out for a walk in the grounds with little Edward. I strolled around to look at that strange side of the house. There were four windows in a row, three of which were just dirty. The fourth had thick shutters covering it. As I strolled up and down, Mr Rucastle came out to me, looking as merry as ever.

"'Ah!" he said, "I apologise if I seemed rude this morning. My mind was stuck on business matters."

"'That's quite all right," I replied with a smile. "By the way," I continued, "you seem to have quite a lot of rooms up there that all seem abandoned. One of them even has the shutters up."

'He looked surprised.

'"Photography is one of my hobbies," he said. "I have made a darkroom up there. But, dear me! What a clever young lady you are. Who would have believed it!" He sounded as if he

Darkroom

A darkroom is used to develop photographs. The windows will all be covered with shutters or thick curtains, to keep the light out. There will usually be large pots of chemicals in a darkroom, that photographs are dipped into. Darkrooms are very private spaces. Photographers do not like people to enter as, if they let light in, the photographs they are developing could be destroyed.

were joking, but there was no laughter in his eyes.

'Well, Mr Holmes, from that moment I knew there was a secret in those rooms. I just had to see in them. It was not just nosiness, I promise. It was more a feeling of duty. I felt in my gut that some good would come from me getting through that forbidden door.'

'It was only yesterday that the chance came. I had seen both Toller and his wife going in and out of those secret rooms. I once even saw him carrying a large

black linen bag through the door.
Yesterday evening, however,
Toller was very drunk. He was
so drunk that he had left the
key in the locked door. Mr and
Mrs Rucastle and Edward were
all downstairs, so I knew it was
the perfect opportunity. I gently
turned the key, opened the door,
and slipped through.'

Chapter Six

Miss Hunter reached for a glass of water.

I was holding my breath, waiting for the next bit of the story. Holmes was sitting forwards in his chair.

'There was a little passage in front of me,' she continued, 'which turned at a right angle at the far end. Around this corner were three doors in a line. The first and third door were open.

They each led into dusty, empty rooms. The windows were so thick with dirt that the evening light shone only dimly through them.

'The centre door was locked shut and had a heavy metal bar across it. I realised that this room must have been the one with the shuttered window. Surprisingly, a little light seeped out from below the door. I concluded that it must have a window in the roof.

'I stood gazing at the door and wondering what secrets it might hold. Suddenly I heard the sound of steps coming from inside the room.

'A mad terror rose up in me, Mr Holmes. My nerves failed me suddenly and I turned and ran as fast as I could. I rushed down the passage, and straight into the arms of Mr Rucastle.

'"So," he said, smiling, "it was you, then. I thought that it must be when I saw the door open."

'"Oh, I am so frightened!" I cried.

'"My dear young lady. What has frightened you?"

'He tried to soothe me, but his voice was just a little too soft. It felt like a clever act.

"'I was foolish enough to go into the empty wing," I answered, carefully. "But it is so lonely and spooky in this dim light that I was frightened and ran out again. Oh, it's so dreadfully still in there!"

"'Only that?' he said, looking at me sharply.

"'Why, what did you think?' I asked.

"'Why do you think that I lock this door?' he replied.

"'I don't know.'

"'It is to keep people out who have no business in there. Do you see?" He was still smiling in a sickly-sweet way.

'"I am sure that if I had known ..."

'"Well you know now. If you ever put your foot inside that doorway again ..." His smile hardened into a grin of rage as he glared down at me. "I'll throw you to the mastiff."

'I was so terrified that I don't remember what I did. I must have rushed past him into my room. Before I knew it, I was lying on my bed and trembling all over.'

She looked at us both and I could see the memory of the terror in her eyes.

'Then I thought of you, Mr Holmes. I could not live there any longer without some advice. I could have run away but my curiosity was as strong as my fear. I made up my mind to send you a telegram, so I put on my hat and cloak and went to the telegraph office. When I returned I felt much better. I even stayed awake half the night, excited at the thought of seeing you.'

Holmes' mouth twitched at her words.

'I had no difficulty in getting permission to come to Winchester this morning, but I must be back before three o'clock. Mr and Mrs Rucastle are going on a visit and will be away all evening, so I must look after Edward.

'Now I have told you of all my adventures, Mr Holmes and Doctor

Watson. Can you tell me what it all means? What should I do?'

Holmes and I had listened spellbound to her amazing story. He now got up and paced up and down the room, his hands in his pockets and a very serious look on his face.

'Is Toller still drunk?' he asked.

'Yes. I heard his wife tell Mrs Rucastle that she could do nothing with him.'

'Good. And the Rucastles are going out tonight?'

'Yes.'

'Is there a cellar with a good, strong lock?'

'Yes, there is.'

'You have acted like a very brave and sensible woman, Miss Hunter. Do you think you could perform one more task? I would not ask you if I didn't think you could do it.'

'I will try. What is it?'

'We shall be at The Copper Beeches by seven o'clock. The Rucastles will be gone by that time, and Toller will, we hope, still be drunk. That only leaves

Mrs Toller. Could you send her into the cellar on an errand and then lock the door after her?'

'Yes, I'll do it.'

'Excellent! That will be a great help. Of course, there is only one explanation. You have been brought here to impersonate someone, and the real person is being kept in the room. That is obvious. As to who this prisoner is, I am sure it must be Mr Ruscastle's daughter, Miss Alice Rucastle. I remember you saying that she has gone to America. You must have been

chosen because you are so much like her in height, figure and the colour of your hair. Her hair had been cut off, possibly because of an illness, so yours had to be cut off too. By curious chance, you found her hair in the drawer.

'The man in the road was probably a friend of hers – maybe her fiancé. By wearing her dress and having the same hair, you made him think you were Miss Rucastle. Then by laughing and waving him away, you made him think that Miss Rucastle no longer cared for him. The dog was obviously let loose at night to stop him from contacting her.'

'Oh, we must help this poor girl! We can't waste any time,' cried our client.

'We must be careful,' replied Holmes. 'We are dealing with a very cunning man. We can do nothing until seven o'clock. At that hour we shall be with you and then it won't be long before we solve the mystery.'

Chapter Seven

As we had promised, we reached
The Copper Beeches at seven o'clock.
The group of beech trees were
enough to show us that it was the
right house, even if Miss Hunter had
not been standing on the doorstep.

'Have you managed it?' asked
Holmes as we entered.

A loud thudding came from
somewhere downstairs.

'Yes, that is Mrs Toller in the cellar,' she said. 'Her husband is snoring on the kitchen rug and Edward is tucked up in his bed. Here are the keys.'

'You have done well indeed!' cried Holmes. 'Now lead the way and we shall soon get to the end of this bad business.'

We went up the stairs, unlocked the door, and followed the passageway round to the locked door. Holmes removed the heavy metal bar and then tried the various keys in the lock, without success. No sound came from within the room.

Holmes looked worried.

'I hope we are not too late,' he said. 'I think, Miss Hunter, that we should go in without you. Now, Watson, put your shoulder to the door and we shall break it down.'

It was an old rickety door and gave way easily. Together we rushed into the room. It was empty. There was no furniture except a lightweight bed, a small table and a basket of clean laundry. The window above was open and the prisoner was gone.

'There has been some wickedness here,' said Holmes. 'Mr Rucastle has guessed Miss Hunter's intentions and has carried his victim off.'

'But how?'

'Through the window in the roof. We shall soon see how he managed it.'

He swung himself up through it and peered out onto the roof. 'Ah, yes,' he cried, 'here's the end of a ladder. He must have climbed down.'

'But that's impossible,' said Miss Hunter, 'the ladder was not there when the Rucastles left.'

'Perhaps he came back and did it,' said Holmes, jumping back down. 'I tell you that he is a clever and dangerous man. I wouldn't be surprised if that were him coming up the stairs now. Watson, it would be a good idea to have your gun ready.'

The words were hardly out of his mouth before a man appeared at the door. He was very fat and burly, with a heavy stick in his hand.

Miss Hunter screamed and shrank against the wall at the sight of Mr Rucastle. Holmes sprang forwards. 'You villain!' he said. 'Where is your daughter?'

The fat man cast his eyes around, then up at the open window.

'I should ask you the same question!' he shrieked. 'You thieves! Spies and thieves! I have caught you, have I? I'll get you!' He turned and clattered down the stairs.

'He's gone for the dog!' cried Miss Hunter.

'I have my gun,' I said.

'Better close the front door,' cried Holmes, and we all rushed down the stairs together. We had hardly reached the hall when we heard the snarling of a dog and then a loud scream. An elderly man with a red face and shaking limbs came staggering out of a side door.

'My god!' he cried. 'Someone has
let the dog loose. It hasn't been fed for
two days. Quick! Or it will be too late!'

Holmes and I rushed out and
around the corner of the house. Toller
hurried behind us.

Chapter Eight

The huge dog had its teeth dug into
Rucastle's neck, pinning him to the
ground. Running up, I shot it with
my gun and it fell over sideways. We
carried Rucastle, with difficulty, into
the house and laid him on the drawing-
room sofa. I did what I could to relieve
his pain. Toller was sent to fetch his
wife and within a few minutes in
walked the tall, gaunt woman.

'Mrs Toller!' cried Miss Hunter.

'Yes, miss. Mr Rucastle let me out of the cellar when he returned. It's a pity you didn't let me know what you were planning because I could have told you it was a waste of time.'

'Ha!' said Holmes, looking at her intently. 'It's clear that you know the truth about this mystery.'

'Yes, I do, sir, and I am ready to tell what I know.'

'Then please sit down and let us hear it, for there are several points I'm still unsure about.'

'I'll explain it all to you,' she said. 'I would have done so sooner if you had let me out of the cellar.

'She was never happy at home, Miss Alice wasn't,' explained Mrs Toller. 'Not since her father married again. But it was never that bad until after she met Mr Fowler at a friend's house. As well as I can learn, Miss Alice was left money in her mother's will. She knew about the money but

she never asked
her father for it.
She just left everything
in Mr Rucastle's hands. He
knew he was safe until she got
married – she would not ask
for the money, of course, but he
was sure any husband would. So
her father thought it best to put
a stop to Miss Alice's and Mr
Fowler's romance.

'He wanted her to sign a
paper to say that whether she
married or not, he could use
her money. When she wouldn't

do it, he kept on badgering her until it made her ill. For six weeks she was at death's door. She recovered at last, but was worn to a shadow and all her beautiful hair had been cut off. It didn't make any difference to Mr Fowler. He stuck to her as true as could be.'

'Ah,' said Holmes, 'so then Mr Rucastle trapped her in that room.'

'Yes, sir.'

'And brought Miss Hunter down from London to trick Mr Fowler into leaving them alone.'

'That's right, sir.'

'But when Mr Fowler finally learned the truth, he wanted to free Miss Rucastle. Perhaps he paid you to take his side and help.'

'Mr Fowler is a very kind and generous gentleman,' said Mrs Toller calmly.

'And he made sure that your husband had plenty of drink in return for a ladder being ready the moment Mr Rucastle had gone out.'

'You have it, sir, just as it happened.'

'Then I'm sure we owe you an apology, Mrs Toller,' said Holmes. 'I see now that you were only trying to help Miss Alice. And you have certainly helped in unravelling this mystery, too.

'Ah, here comes the county doctor and Mrs Rucastle. So I think, Watson, that our work here is done. We had better escort Miss Hunter back home.'

Chapter Nine

As Holmes and I sat gazing out of the window after breakfast the next morning, I asked him about Miss Hunter. 'Do you think you will see Miss Hunter again, my dear Holmes?'

'I should not think so. It would be rather clumsy of her to get caught up in yet another troubling mystery,' he replied.

'Well, yes. But perhaps you could visit her on a social call,' I suggested.

Holmes chuckled. 'Ah Watson – always the romantic. Difficult men do not make good husbands. Think of Mrs Rucastle, forever attached to that horrid husband of hers. Or Mrs Toller, the wife of a drunkard. The only pair to have gained from this strange adventure are Mr Fowler and Miss Alice Rucastle. Though, even there we cannot be sure – we will never know if they are happy in their new marriage. No, Watson, such silly things as social calls would only distract me from my work.'

Sherlock Holmes

World-renowned private
detective Sherlock Holmes has
solved hundreds of mysteries,
and is the author of such
fascinating monographs as
Early English Charters and *The
Influence of a Trade Upon the Form of
a Hand.* He keeps bees in his free time.

Dr John Watson

Wounded in action at Maiwand,
Dr John Watson left the army and
moved into 221B Baker Street. There
he was surprised to learn that his
new friend, Sherlock Holmes, faced
daily peril solving crimes, and began
documenting his investigations.
Dr Watson also runs a doctor's practice.

To download Sherlock Holmes activities, please visit
www.sweetcherrypublishing.com/resources